The Magic Watering Can

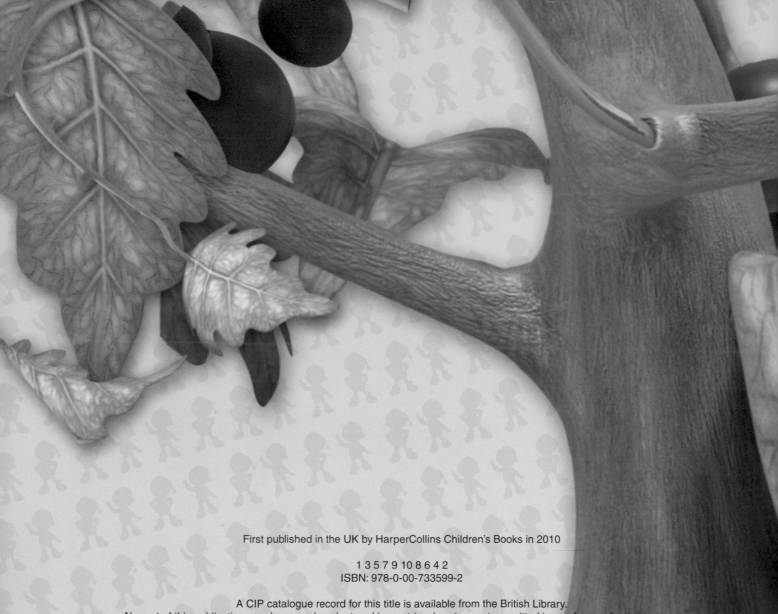

First published in the UK by HarperCollins Children's Books in 2010

1 3 5 7 9 10 8 6 4 2
ISBN: 978-0-00-733599-2

Printed and bound in China

The Magic Watering Can

HarperCollins *Children's Books*

It was a hot, sunny day and
Noddy was helping Big Ears in the
garden at Toadstool House.

"It's kind of you to help me
on such a warm day, Noddy,"
said Big Ears, gratefully.

"That's okay, Big Ears,
this is fun!" said Noddy, as he
used his watering can to water
all the pretty plants.

Even Bumpy wanted to help.
He ran round and round the garden.

"Oh, Bumpy!" laughed Noddy.
"Try not to dig too many holes!"

Bumpy decided to have a rest,
as it was such a sunny day.

"All this sun and water must be good for your plants,
Big Ears – they're really great!" said Noddy.

"I give them a little help with my magic watering can,"
said Big Ears. "I never use too much magic, though!"

Noddy watched in amazement as the plants sprung up from little shoots to lovely, big flowers.

"That's magic!"

gasped Noddy. "What a wonderful watering can you have, Big Ears."

Suddenly, Noddy had an idea.

"Could I borrow your watering can, Big Ears?" he asked, excitedly.
"I've just thought of a brilliant surprise for Tessie!"

"Of course you can," said Big Ears.
"Remember to use just a drop of water, Noddy…"

12

But Noddy didn't hear Big Ears,
as he drove off with Bumpy.

Vroom!
Parp!

"Tessie will be surprised when I show her the magic
watering can," said Noddy, smiling.

It was such a hot day, that Noddy decided to
buy some lemonade to take to Tessie's.

It seemed like everyone in Toyland
had the same idea! They all wanted a nice cold drink,
as it was so warm and sunny.

"Lots of cool lemonade, please,
Mr Wobbly Man," said Noddy.

"Brrr!
That's perfect!"

Just then, Mr Jumbo appeared.
"I'd like a lemonade, too, please!" he bellowed.

"Coming up!" said Mr Wobbly Man.
"Why don't you sit in the shade while you drink it?"

"There's not much shade to fit under," said Mr Jumbo,
flapping his ears to keep cool.

16

When Noddy arrived at Tessie's house,
they sat down to enjoy their drinks.

"This lemonade is a lovely surprise, Noddy,"
said Tessie. "You must try some of my fairy cakes.
They'll be ready soon."

"Fairy Cakes! Yum! Oh, and I have another
surprise for you, Tessie!" said Noddy.

Noddy waved Big Ears' magic watering can in the air.
"It's MAGIC, Tessie!" said Noddy. "Watch this!"

Noddy started to sprinkle water all over
Tessie's pretty tomato plants.

The plants didn't seem to get any bigger,
so Noddy kept on watering them.

"Hmmm…it worked for Big Ears," he said, with a puzzled look. "Perhaps they need even more water."

Noddy kept on sprinkling.
Then suddenly, Tessie's tomato plants started to

grow...
and grow...
and GROW!

"Oh no, Noddy," said Tessie. "The plants are so big they are blocking my door and my fairy cakes are still baking in the oven!"

"Don't worry, Tessie!" cried Noddy. "I've got a big Noddy plan!"

He called for Lindy and Car.

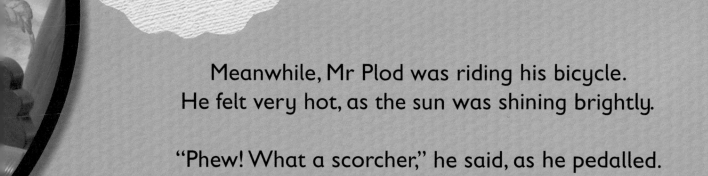

Meanwhile, Mr Plod was riding his bicycle.
He felt very hot, as the sun was shining brightly.

"Phew! What a scorcher," he said, as he pedalled.
Just then, he spotted the very big plant in front of Tessie's
house. He turned his head and stared…

Crash! Boing! Splash!

Mr Plod toppled off his bicycle and into the pond!

"Well, that's cooled me down a bit!" he chuckled.
"But what's little Noddy up to now?"

Noddy was climbing up the tomato plant,
which was now as big as a tree.

He looked down and saw that Lindy
had arrived to help him.

"I'm going to start cutting away the leaves so that Tessie can get into her house," Noddy explained. "Car will catch them for me!"

"Good idea, Noddy!"

said Lindy, as she hovered next to him.

When Noddy had finished, he climbed back down to Tessie.
Big Ears had just arrived.

"I wanted to warn you not to use too much of my watering
can's magic, Noddy," said Big Ears. "But I think I'm too late!"

"Don't worry, Big Ears," said Noddy. "The extra-big leaves
are very useful on this hot and sunny day!"

The giant leaves made great parasols for
all the Toy Town friends.

"I'm nice and cool now," said Mr Jumbo, as he held up his leaf.

Dinah Doll, the Skittles and Clockwork Mouse all agreed.
"Clever, Noddy!" they said, as they stayed cool.

Tessie was very happy,
as her fairy cakes were saved!
But what were they going to do
with the giant tomatoes that had
piled up outside?

"I have an idea!" said Noddy,
"We'll have a spaghetti party!"

So they sat down and shared a
plate of tasty spaghetti.

Slurp!
Yum!
Slurp!

"What delicious tomato sauce!"
they both agreed.

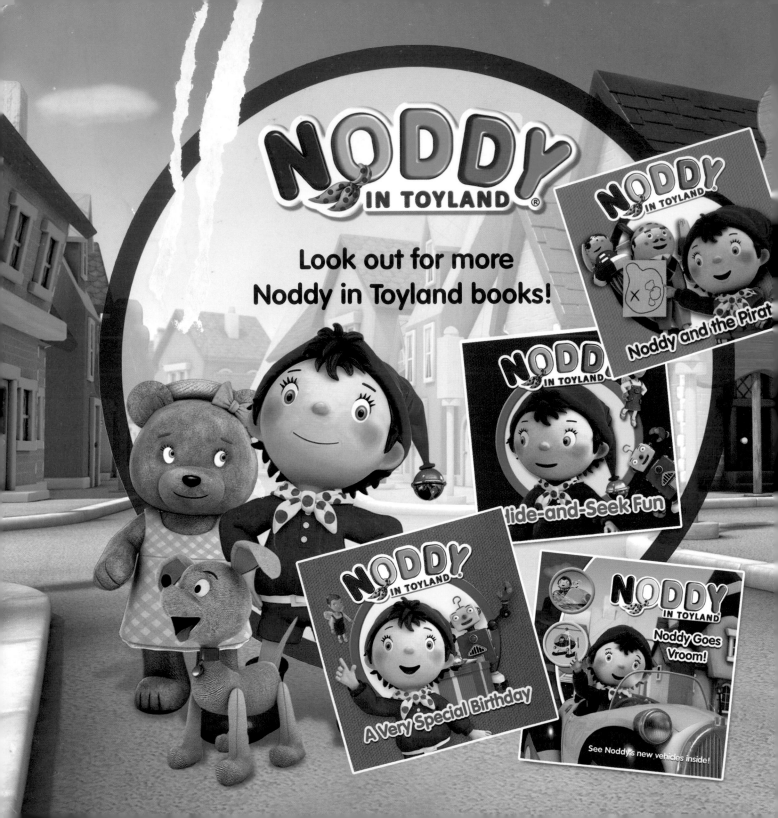